A Note to Parents

Welcome to REAL KIDS READERS, a series of phonics-based books for children who are beginning to read. In the classroom, educators use phonics to teach children how to sound out unfamiliar words, providing a firm foundation for reading skills. At home, you can use REAL KIDS READERS to reinforce and build on that foundation, because the books follow the same basic phonic guidelines that children learn in school.

Of course the best way to help your child become a good reader is to make the experience fun—and REAL KIDS READERS do that, too. With their realistic story lines and lively characters, the books engage children's imaginations. With their clean design and sparkling photographs, they provide picture clues that help new readers decipher the text. The combination is sure to entertain young children and make them truly want to read.

REAL KIDS READERS have been developed at three distinct levels to make it easy for children to read at their own pace.

- LEVEL 1 is for children who are just beginning to read.
- LEVEL 2 is for children who can read with help.
- LEVEL 3 is for children who can read on their own.

A controlled vocabulary provides the framework at each level. Repetition, rhyme, and humor help increase word skills. Because children can understand the words and follow the stories, they quickly develop confidence. They go back to each book again and again, increasing their proficiency and sense of accomplishment, until they're ready to move on to the next level. The result is a rich and rewarding experience that will help them develop a lifelong love of reading.

This book is for Bridgie and for Luke,
and in memory of the Tiger Stripe Band
—M. B.

Special thanks to Charles Hunter and St. Luke's School,
New York City, for use of the children's instruments.

Produced by DWAI / Seventeenth Street Productions, Inc.
Reading Specialist: Virginia Grant Clammer

Library of Congress Cataloging-in-Publication Data
Bernstein, Margery.
  Stop that noise! / Margery Bernstein ; photographs by Dorothy Handelman.
       p.   cm. — (Real kids readers. Level 3)
  Summary: Three children who love to make music in inappropriate places are organized by
their teacher into a band to perform at their school's open house.
  ISBN 0-7613-2060-1 (lib. bdg.). — ISBN 0-7613-2085-7 (pbk.)
  [1. Noise—Fiction. 2. Bands (Music)—Fiction. 3. Schools—Fiction.] I. Handelman, Dorothy,
ill. II. Title. III. Series.
PZ7.B4567St   1999
[E]—dc21
                                                           98-38107
                                                           CIP
                                                           AC

pbk: 10 9 8 7 6 5 4 3 2 1
lib: 10 9 8 7 6 5 4 3 2 1

Stop That Noise!

By Margery Bernstein

Photographs by Dorothy Handelman

The Millbrook Press

Brookfield, Connecticut

Rat-a-tat. Rat-a-tat. Mike tapped his pencil on his school desk. *Rat-a-tat. Rat-a-tat-tat-tat!*

This did not make his teacher happy. "Mike! Please stop that noise!" said Mr. Patterson. "This is *silent* reading time, remember?"

"Sorry," said Mike. He put down his pencil. He *had* been reading. But he could tap and read at the same time— no problem. It was harder for him *not* to tap.

Mike liked to make his own music. He kept two drumsticks in his back-pack. On his way home from school, he took them out. Then he tapped out the beat he heard in his head.

He dragged his sticks along fences. He drummed on mailboxes and garbage cans. Once he even drummed on a car! But then a woman yelled at him, so he never did that again.

When Mike got home, he didn't put his sticks away. There were lots of places in the house where he could make music. The kitchen was the best.

First he drummed on the stove. Then he tapped on the kitchen table. Then he banged on some pots and pans.

What a great sound *they* made!

Mike's mom came into the kitchen. "Mike!" she said. "Please stop that noise! The banging is driving me crazy."

Mike didn't want to drive his mom crazy. He didn't want to make her mad either. So he put his sticks away. But the beat still went on in his head.

He used a spoon to tap it out on his soup bowl at dinner. He used a duster to tap it out on his globe when he was supposed to be cleaning his room. He used his toothbrush to tap it out on the sink at bedtime.

With Mike around, nothing was safe. He'd use *any* surface to make his music.

Mike had a friend named Sara. She had a great voice, and she liked to sing—anywhere, anytime.

She sang in the living room when her sister was trying to read.

"Stop that noise!" said her sister.

She sang in the family room when her brother was trying to watch TV.

"Stop that noise!" said her brother.

She sang at the dinner table with her mouth full of mashed potatoes.

This did not make her parents happy.

"Sara!" said her mom. "Don't sing at the table with mashed potatoes in your mouth."

Sara swallowed her potatoes. She opened her mouth to sing.

"Sara!" said her dad. "Don't sing at the table *without* mashed potatoes in your mouth. In fact, please keep your mouth closed."

After that, Sara kept her mouth closed when she was around other people. But tunes kept playing in her head, so she hummed.

She hummed as she chose books at the library. She hummed during soccer practice. She hummed while she got her hair cut.

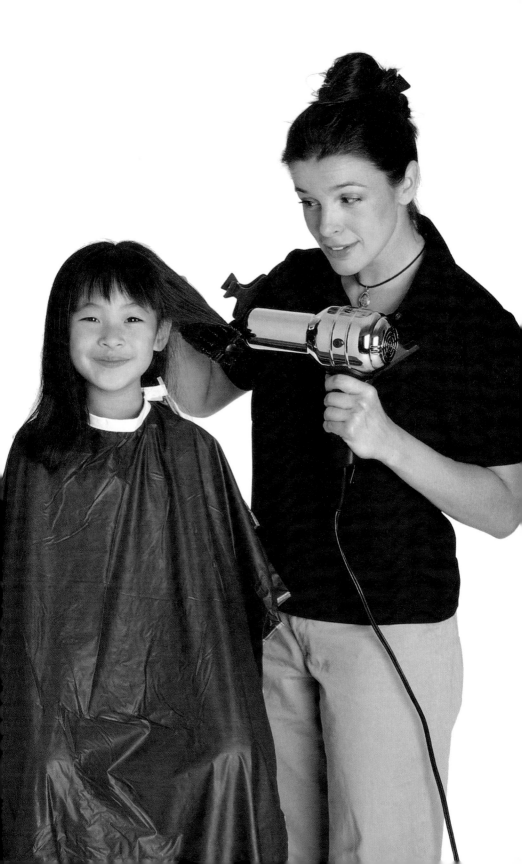

She hummed in school.

"Sara, are you listening to me?" asked Mr. Patterson. "Are you paying attention?"

"Yes," said Sara.

"Then please tell me what I just said," said Mr. Patterson.

"You said, 'Sara, are you listening to me? Are you paying attention?'" said Sara.

Mr. Patterson sighed.

Mike and Sara had a friend named Tom. His head was full of music too. But he didn't drum or hum. He made sounds in other ways.

He zipped his jacket up and down. He jingled coins in his pocket. He ran his fingers down the teeth of his comb.

24

Tom knew you could make music with almost anything. You could blow across the top of a bottle to make a low, deep sound. Or you could let air out of a balloon to make a high, squeaky sound.

This did not make his family happy.

"Hey! Stop that noise!" yelled his big sister. "I'm trying to talk on the phone."

Tom didn't have a flute or a horn or any other *real* instrument. So he made his own music makers.

He made one by putting dried beans in an empty salt box and shaking it. He made another by folding waxed paper over a comb and blowing on it. And he made another by filling glasses with water and tapping them with a spoon.

Sometimes Tom made music at school. One day, during silent reading, he took out a rubber band. He stretched it between his thumb and little finger on one hand. Then he strummed it with his other hand. *Twang, twang, twang.*

From across the room came a *rat-a-tat-tat* as Mike tapped his pencil to the beat. Then Sara joined in, humming softly.

"I just can't believe it," thought Mr. Patterson. "A drummer, a hummer, and a strummer—all in my class. How did I get so lucky?"

He was about to tell the three kids to stop the noise. But then he stopped to listen—*really* listen. What he heard wasn't noise. It was . . . music!

That gave him an idea.

"Mike, Tom, Sara, " Mr. Patterson called. "Please step into the hall with me a moment."

"Uh-oh," said Mike.
"We're in trouble," said Tom.
"*Big* trouble," said Sara. Slowly, they
followed Mr. Patterson from the room.

"Listen," said Mr. Patterson. "I can tell that music is important to you. But I can't let you disturb the other kids. So here's the deal. *If* you promise to keep quiet during class, I'll help you form a band. *If* it's okay with your parents, you can practice here after school. And *if* you stick with it, you can play at the school open house."

He smiled at the kids. "So how about it? Do we have a deal?"

"Yes!" said Sara.

"It's a deal," said Mike.

"It's a *good* deal," said Tom.

The open house was only two weeks away. Mike, Sara, and Tom practiced every day after school to get ready.

They tried new ways to make music. They made new instruments. They listened to one another and worked hard together. They even came up with a name for the band.

They also helped one another keep their promise.

If Mike forgot and started tapping his pencil, Tom hit him with a rubber band. If Tom forgot and started strumming, Sara cleared her throat loudly. And if Sara forgot and started humming, Mike tapped her with his pencil.

Finally it was the night of the open house. Parents sat at their kids' desks. They looked at their kids' schoolwork. They asked lots of questions.

Afterward Mr. Patterson said, "I have a special treat. Our own class band will perform for you tonight. Please welcome—Good Deal!"

Mike, Tom, and Sara marched into the room. They were nervous, but they were proud too.

41

They began to play. First Mike set the beat with his drum. Then Sara began to sing, keeping time with a pair of shakers. Then Tom joined in with his music makers.

Tom's parents smiled. Sara's parents hummed along with the music. Mike's parents tapped their feet. All of the grown-ups were amazed. The band was really good!

The kids looked at one another and grinned. They were doing what they liked to do best—making music. And no one was saying "Stop that noise" now!

Reading with Your Child

Even though your child is reading more independently now, it is vital that you continue to take part in this important learning experience.

- Try to read with your child at least twenty minutes each day, as part of your regular routine.
- Encourage your child to keep favorite books in one convenient, cozy spot, so you don't waste valuable reading time looking for them.
- Read and familiarize yourself with the Phonic Guidelines on the next pages.
- Praise your young reader. Be the cheerleader, not the teacher. Your enthusiasm and encouragement are key ingredients in your child's success.

What to Do if Your Child Gets Stuck on a Word

- Wait a moment to see if he or she works it out alone.
- Help him or her decode the word phonetically. Say, "Try to sound it out."
- Encourage him or her to use picture clues. Say, "What does the picture show?"
- Encourage him or her to use context clues. Say, "What would make sense?"
- Ask him or her to try again. Say, "Read the sentence again and start the tricky word. Get your mouth ready to say it."
- If your child still doesn't "get" the word, tell him or her what it is. Don't wait for frustration to build.

What to Do if Your Child Makes a Mistake

- If the mistake makes sense, ignore it—unless it is part of a pattern of errors you wish to correct.
- If the mistake doesn't make sense, wait a moment to see if your child corrects it.
- If your child doesn't correct the mistake, ask him or her to try again, either by decoding the word or by using context or picture clues. Say, "Get your mouth ready" or "Make it sound right" or "Make it make sense."
- If your child still doesn't "get" the word, tell him or her what it is. Don't wait for frustration to build.

Phonic Guidelines

Use the following guidelines to help your child read the words in this story.

Short Vowels

When two consonants surround a vowel, the sound of the vowel is usually short. This means you pronounce *a* as in apple, *e* as in egg, *i* as in igloo, *o* as in octopus, and *u* as in umbrella. Words with short vowels include: *bed, big, box, cat, cup, dad, dog, get, hid, hop, hum, jam, kid, mad, met, mom, pen, ran, sad, sit, sun, top.*

R-Controlled Vowels

When a vowel is followed by the letter *r*, its sound is changed by the *r*. Words with *r*-controlled vowels include: *card, curl, dirt, farm, girl, herd, horn, jerk, torn, turn.*

Long Vowel and Silent E

If a word has a vowel followed by a consonant and an *e*, usually the vowel is long and the *e* is silent. Long vowels are pronounced the same way as their alphabet names. Words with a long vowel and silent *e* include: *bake, cute, dive, game, home, kite, mule, page, pole, ride, vote.*

Double Vowels

When two vowels are side by side, usually the first vowel is long and the second vowel is silent. Words with double vowels include: *boat, clean, gray, loaf, meet, neat, paint, pie, play, rain, sleep, tried.*

Diphthongs

Sometimes when two vowels (or a vowel and a consonant) are side by side, they combine to make a diphthong—a sound that is different from long or short vowel sounds. Diphthongs are: *au/aw, ew, oi/oy, ou/ow.* Words with diphthongs include: *auto, brown, claw, flew, found, join, toy.*

Double Consonants

When two identical consonants appear side by side, one of them is silent. Words with double consonants include: *bell, fuss, mess, mitt, puff, tall, yell.*

Consonant Blends

When two or more different consonants are side by side, they usually blend to make a combined sound. Words with consonant blends include: *bent, blob, bride, club, crib, drop, flip, frog, gift, glare, grip, help, jump, mask, most, pink, plane, ring, send, skate, sled, spin, steep, swim, trap, twin.*

Consonant Digraphs
Sometimes when two different consonants are side by side, they make a digraph that represents a single new sound. Consonant digraphs are: *ch, sh, th, wh*. Words with digraphs include: *bath, chest, lunch, sheet, think, whip, wish*.

Silent Consonants
Sometimes, when two different consonants are side by side, one of them is silent. Words with silent consonants include: *back, dumb, knit, knot, lamb, sock, walk, wrap, wreck*.

Sight Words
Sight words are those words that a reader must learn to recognize immediately—by sight—instead of by sounding them out. They occur with high frequency in easy texts. Sight words include: *a, am, an, and, as, at, be, big, but, can, come, do, for, get, give, have, he, her, his, I, in, is, it, just, like, look, make, my, new, no, not, now, old, one, out, play, put, red, run, said, see, she, so, some, soon, that, the, then, there, they, to, too, two, under, up, us, very, want, was, we, went, what, when, where, with, you*.

Exceptions to the "Rules"
Although much of the English language is phonically regular, there are many words that don't follow the above guidelines. For example, a particular combination of letters can represent more than one sound. Double *oo* can represent a long *oo* sound, as in words such as *boot, cool,* and *moon;* or it can represent a short *oo* sound, as in words such as *foot, good,* and *hook*. The letters *ow* can represent a diphthong, as in words such as *brow, fowl,* and *town;* or they can represent a long *o* sound, as in words such as *blow, snow,* and *tow*. Additionally, some high-frequency words such as *some, come, have,* and *said* do not follow the guidelines at all, and *ough* appears in such different-sounding words as *although, enough,* and *thought*.

The phonic guidelines provided in this book are just that—guidelines. They do not cover all the irregularities in our rich and varied language, but are intended to correspond roughly to the phonic lessons taught in the first and second grades. Phonics provides the foundation for learning to read. Repetition, visual clues, context, and sheer experience provide the rest.

I have read these Real Kids Readers:

Level 1
- Big Ben
- The Big Box
- Dan and Dan
- Dress-Up
- Get the Ball, Slim
- Hop, Skip, Run
- I Like Mess
- Mud!
- My Camp-Out
- My Pal Al
- The New Kid
- The Pet Vet
- Spots
- The Tin Can Man

Level 2
- The Best Pet Yet
- The Big Sale
- Did You Hear About Jake?
- The Good Bad Day
- Lost and Found
- The Lunch Bunch
- Monster Songs
- My Brother, the Pest
- The Rainy Day Grump
- Shoes, Shoes, Shoes
- Show and Tell
- That Cat!
- That's Hard, That's Easy
- Too-Tall Paul, Too-Small Paul

Level 3
- Lemonade for Sale
- Loose-Tooth Luke
- Molly in the Middle
- My Pen Pal, Pat
- On with the Show!
- Stop That Noise!
- That Is *Not* My Hat!
- You're in Big Trouble, Brad!

DISCARD

REAL KIDS READERS™

Stop That Noise!

LEVEL 3 Grade 1 to Grade

Mike drums on any surface. Sara hums all day. Tom makes all kinds of odd sounds. They drive their families crazy and disturb their class-mates. How can their teacher stop that noise?

"A welcome new series for the earliest readers."

School Library Journal

"Real Kids Readers are a welcome resource for helping children become skilled readers. These appealing books engage the young reader with realistic story lines and lively characters; most important, they provide needed opportunities for practicing and reinforcing essential phonic skills and sight vocabulary taught in school."

Alvin Granowsky, Ed.D.
(Dr. Granowsky has served as the Reading Consultant to the National PTA and as Director of Reading for the public schools of Greensboro, NC, and Dallas, TX.)

Level 1: Ages 4 to 6 Preschool to Grade 1
Level 2: Ages 5 to 7 Kindergarten to Grade 2
Level 3: Ages 6 to 8 Grade 1 to Grade 3

REAL KIDS READERS

$3.99 U.S./Higher in Canada

ISBN 0-7613-2085-7

90000>

EAN

9 780761 320852

M

THE MILLBROOK PRESS

YOKO & FRIENDS
SCHOOL DAYS

Read Me a Story

ROSEMARY WELLS

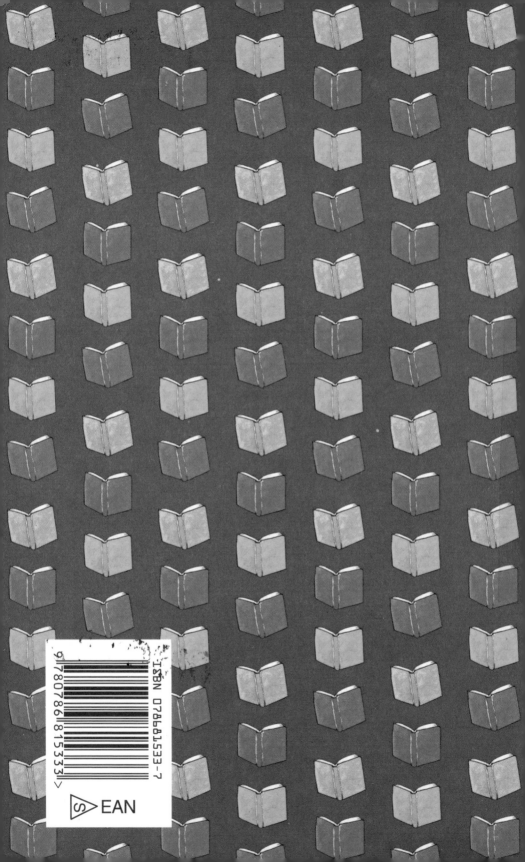

ISBN 0-7613-1533-7